Have Yourself a *Scary* Little Christmas . . .

Kenny Frobisher is the biggest, meanest bully ever. He'll do anything he can to ruin Christmas for everyone in Shadyside.

Until he gets himself trapped in a closet in Dalby's Department Store on Christmas Eve.

When Kenny finally gets out, the store is dark. Empty. Deserted. Kenny's all alone. Until the three most frightening ghosts of Fear Street arrive . . .

And show Kenny what happens to children who are *really* naughty.

Also from R. L. Stine

The Beast
The Beast 2

R. L. Stine's Ghosts of Fear Street
 #1 Hide and Shriek
 #2 Who's Been Sleeping in My Grave?
 #3 Attack of the Aqua Apes
 #4 Nightmare in 3-D
 #5 Stay Away from the Tree House
 #6 Eye of the Fortuneteller
 #7 Fright Knight
 #8 The Ooze
 #9 Revenge of the Shadow People
#10 The Bugman Lives!
#11 The Boy Who Ate Fear Street
#12 Night of the Werecat
#13 How to Be a Vampire
#14 Body Switchers from Outer Space

Available from MINSTREL Books

R·L·STINE'S
GHOSTS of FEAR STREET ®

FRIGHT
CHRISTMAS

A Parachute Press Book

A
MINSTREL ®
BOOK

PUBLISHED BY POCKET BOOKS

New York   London   Toronto   Sydney   Tokyo   Singapore

This book is a work of fiction. Names, characters, places and incidents are products of the author's imagination or are used fictitiously. Any resemblance to actual events or locales or persons, living or dead, is entirely coincidental.

A MINSTREL PAPERBACK *Original*

 A Minstrel Paperback published by
POCKET BOOKS, a division of Simon & Schuster Inc.
1230 Avenue of the Americas, New York, NY 10020

Copyright © 1996 by Parachute Press, Inc.

FRIGHT CHRISTMAS WRITTEN BY STEPHEN ROOS

All rights reserved, including the right to reproduce
this book or portions thereof in any form whatsoever.
For information address Pocket Books, 1230 Avenue
of the Americas, New York, NY 10020

ISBN: 0-671-00187-6

First Minstrel Books paperback printing December 1996

10 9 8 7 6 5 4 3 2 1

FEAR STREET is a registered trademark of
Parachute Press, Inc.

A MINSTREL BOOK and colophon are registered trademarks
of Simon & Schuster Inc.

Cover art by John Youssi

Printed in the U.S.A.

FRIGHT
CHRISTMAS

"Kenny, look!" My little sister's face lit up with a big smile. She held up a ballerina doll for me to see. "Isn't she beautiful?" She sighed. "This is the one I want for Christmas."

My mom took Kristi to see the ballet *Sleeping Beauty* last month. Now that's all she talks about, all day long. Ballerinas. Ballerinas. Ballerinas.

"Are you sure this is the one you want?" I asked her.

Kristi's head bobbed up and down. "Oh, yes!" she said.

"Let's see if she can twirl." I took the doll from Kristi and spun her around on her head.

"Kenny! Stop. You're ruining her hair," Kristi wailed.

The doll spun to a stop. She fell flat on her back and her eyelids jammed shut.

"Look, Kristi. She *is* the one you want," I exclaimed. "She can be Sleeping Beauty."

I tossed the doll on a shelf.

"Kenny! Give her back to me!" Kristi brushed her short blond curls from her face. "I have to show her to Santa—so he'll know what to bring me for Christmas."

Christmas.

That's why I was stuck here—in the middle of Dalby's Department Store. On Christmas Eve. In the toy department. With Santa and his dumb elves and my six-year-old sister, Kristi.

It's not that I have anything against Christmas. I mean I like the presents—it's all the "peace on earth" stuff I hate.

Anyway, Mom said I had to watch Kristi while she finished up her Christmas shopping—which ruined my whole night.

I think Christmas Eve is the best night of the year. It's when I sneak into our neighbors' yards—and unscrew all the lightbulbs on their Christmas trees.

Kristi tugged on my sleeve. "Come on, Kenny.

We have to get in line to meet Santa. I have to sit on his lap and tell him what I want."

"Santa had to go back to the North Pole," I told her. "We can't see him. He's not here anymore."

Someone tapped me on the shoulder.

Uh-oh. I hope it's not Mom. I hope she didn't hear me just lie to Kristi. I'll be in for it big-time.

It wasn't Mom. It was worse.

Timmy Smathers. A real nerd. And the shortest kid from my class at Shadyside Middle School.

"Hi, Kenny!" Timmy greeted me with his big goofy smile. "Isn't this toy department awesome?"

I stared at him blankly for a second. Then I glanced down at him and said, "Oh, Timmy—it's you. For a second I thought you were one of Santa's elves.

Timmy's smile faded from his face. He hates when anyone mentions his height. So I do it as much as I can.

"Hi, Kristi!" Timmy turned to my sister. "Did you tell Santa what you want for Christmas?" he asked in his squeaky little voice.

Kristi shook her head. She peered down at her sneakers.

"Santa isn't here anymore. He had to go back to the North Pole," she whispered. "Kenny said so."

Then she glanced up at me. Her lower lip trembled. I spotted a big fat tear slide out of the corner of her eye and down her cheek.

"Hey! Don't cry, Kristi." Timmy smiled his goofy smile again. "Kenny made a mistake. Santa is sitting in his village right now. He won't leave until all the kids get a turn to talk to him."

Kristi's face turned beet red. She scrunched up her nose—her angry look.

"You lied to me, Kenny!" she yelled. "Take me to Santa's Village. Right now!"

"Bye, Kenny. Merry Christmas!" Timmy shouted cheerfully as he strolled away from us.

"Bye, Tiny. I mean Timmy," I called back. "Merry Christmas!"

"If you don't take me right now, I'm telling Mom how you lied to me about Santa," Kristi threatened.

"Okay! We're going. Come on," I groaned.

I grabbed Kristi's hand and tugged her toward the end of the toy department—to Santa's Village.

Santa's Village. The stupidest place I ever saw. A big sign at the entrance said: SANTA'S STREET! FILLED WITH TOYS—FOR ALL GOOD LITTLE GIRLS AND BOYS!

At each side of the entrance stood two tall wooden soldiers. Big plastic structures, painted to look like gingerbread houses, lined the street inside

4

the entrance. They were dusted with fake snow. Icicles hung from their rooftops.

We walked through a little white gate and stood in line with the other kids.

I craned my neck to see up ahead.

At the very end of Santa Street, I spotted the jolly fat man himself. He sat in a big gold sleigh decorated with thick red satin ribbons and big golden bells.

A little boy sat on Santa's lap and whispered in the old guy's ear. "Ho-ho-ho!" Santa boomed. His voice sounded totally fake.

Boy, what a lame Santa. I can't believe these little kids don't catch on.

The line crept forward slowly.

Santa's elves ran up and down Santa Street, ringing their annoying bells and handing out candy canes. They tried to make everyone sing Christmas carols with them.

Kristi sang along in her squeaky little voice, happily sucking on a candy cane.

"How long until we get to the front, Kenny?" she asked between licks on her candy cane. "I can't wait to see Santa."

"How old are you now, Kristi?"

"I'm six, Kenny, and you know it!" she exclaimed.

"Well, by the time you get to sit on Santa's lap, you'll be about eight," I told her.

"Ken-nnny," Kristi groaned. She turned and stared longingly at Santa. Her little blond curls bounced around her face.

Mom says my hair looked just like that when I was six. Yuck! I'm glad I've got normal hair now—straight, regular brown hair.

And I'm glad I'm really tall—not short like Tiny Timmy. Or these stupid elves, I thought as one tried to shove a candy cane into my hand.

"Hey, Kristi," I leaned over and whispered. "I bet I know something about Santa that you don't know."

"Leave me alone, Kenny," she sniffed.

"But it's about Santa," I said. "It's a secret. It's really important."

She turned her head and peered up at me through narrowed eyes. I could tell I'd made her curious.

"What about him?" she asked.

"That guy up there is *not* the real Santa," I whispered.

"He is too!" she shot back.

"Nope." I shook my head seriously. "He isn't."

"He is!" Kristi insisted. Her eyes grew round and her lower lip quivered.

"He is what?" Mom asked, coming up behind us.

"Kenny says—" Kristi started to say.

One of the elves rang a golden bell. "It's your turn, little girl." He smiled brightly at Kristi.

Phew! Saved by the bell, I laughed to myself.

The elf led Kristi up to Santa's sleigh. Two other elves hoisted her up onto Santa's lap.

Kristi's blue eyes sparkled as bright as Christmas-tree lights. I never saw a little kid so happy.

This was going to be great.

I strolled up to the sleigh and stood behind my mother. She watched Kristi, smiling and waving.

She'd never even notice if I disappeared.

"Ho-ho-ho!" Santa bellowed as Kristi settled on his lap. "What's your name, little girl?"

I slipped through the crowd to the far end of the sleigh.

I darted past a few elves and stood there, pretending to watch Kristi.

"Kristi Frobisher," Kristi replied happily. "I live at 27 Fear Street. It's the fourth house on the left. It has blue shutters and two big chimneys and—"

"That's okay, Kristi. Santa will find it," he promised. "And what would you like me to bring you for Christmas, dear?"

I peered around.

Everyone had their eyes glued to Santa.

I dropped down to the floor and slipped under the sleigh.

I slithered along the floor on my belly.

Up above, I heard Kristi chattering away. Kristi and Santa sat directly overhead now.

I stopped and crawled out—behind the sleigh. The fur-trimmed edge of Santa's red jacket hung inches from my face. The fur tickled my nose. I sucked in a sneeze.

"But what I really want is a ballerina doll," Kristi droned on. "She's got blond hair and a pink tutu and satin toe shoes. And when you press a button on her back, she . . ."

Perfect timing!

I jumped up.

Santa turned to face me. His fluffy white eyebrows arched in surprise.

I reached out.

With both hands, I grabbed Santa's big white beard.

And I pulled with all my might!

2

"**H**ey!" Santa shouted.

He yanked his head back.

Great! He's helping me.

While Santa pulled his head one way, I tugged his beard the opposite way.

Before you could say "Ho! Ho! Ho!" Santa's hands flew up to hide his pale, bare face.

"He's a fake!" I yelled out. I waved the long white beard over my head for everyone to see. "A big fake! Now do you believe me, Kristi?"

Kristi stood up in the sleigh and stared at me. Her mouth hung open in shock. "You're so mean, Kenny!" she wailed.

"Kenny!" Mom cried. "How could you *do that!*"

All along Santa Street the little kids sobbed and whimpered.

"What happened to Santa?" one little boy cried out.

"I want the *real* Santa!" another one shrieked.

The grown-ups tried to shush them up. The elves ran around frantically, ringing their bells and doling out handfuls of candy.

What a riot!

"You rotten kid!" Santa yelled at me. "Give me back that beard!"

He grabbed for the beard. But I snatched it out of his reach. He lost his balance and nearly toppled out of the sleigh. When he sat up, he glared at me.

I knew that look. He wanted to wring my neck.

I stared at the beardless Santa. He looked really familiar.

Joe! The custodian at Shadyside Middle School. Sure, it had to be!

"Hey, Joe!" I laughed at him. "How did you get to be Santa Claus?"

"You always were a rotten kid, Frobisher," he groaned. "And you always will be."

Scowling, he grabbed his beard back from me. He pressed it to his cheeks, but it didn't stick.

"Come on, Joe," I chuckled. "It was just a joke."

"See anyone laughing, Kenny?" he asked.

"How could anyone do that to these little children?" a salesperson grumbled.

"He should be ashamed of himself," another man agreed.

"He's a dreadful boy," a tall woman muttered as she glared at me. "No—not a boy. A monster."

A quick-thinking elf stood up on the sleigh and called everyone to attention. "Don't worry, folks. Santa is just fine. His beard is magic, you know. Sometimes Santa has to take it off—so he won't be recognized."

The little kids believed him. They wiped their eyes and stopped crying.

Behind the sleigh, another elf helped Joe glue his beard back in place.

"Now, if you'll just get back in line, boys and girls," the elf on the sleigh announced, "you can still tell Santa what you want for Christmas."

"Kenny!" My mother's sharp, angry voice rang out from the other side of the sleigh. "Come over here—this instant!"

Kristi grinned for the first time all night.

I gulped.

"Be there in a few minutes, Mom." I had to slip away. Hide someplace. Until Mom had time to cool off a little. Mom cools off pretty fast.

But where could I go?

I made my way around the back of the sleigh—and spotted a door. A sign hung on it. In big, bold red letters it said: DANGER! KEEP OUT! AUTHORIZED PERSONNEL ONLY.

Talk about a lucky break!

I'll duck in here for ten minutes. When I come out, Mom will be in a hurry to get home. She won't have time to yell at me—at least not much.

I could hear Santa greeting the crowd again from up on the sleigh.

I glanced over at Mom. She and Kristi were studying a display of ballerina dolls.

Nobody else was looking at me either.

Great! A perfect time for my escape.

I tiptoed over to the door.

I turned the doorknob.

Yes! It was my lucky break! The door wasn't locked.

I quietly slipped inside the small room.

I quickly pulled the door closed behind me—and gasped.

What a room!

Floor-to-ceiling computers filled each wall—with hundreds of switches and buttons. Every inch of wall space was covered with them—switches, buttons, levers, and dials—all lit with tiny lights in a zillion different colors. Glowing and blinking lights—brighter and better than any Christmas tree I'd ever seen.

I heard a low hum coming from all directions. And through the soles of my sneakers I felt the floor softly vibrate.

Wow! This is like the space-capsule simulator ride at AstroLand. Only this was better.

And here I was. In the middle of it all. By myself.

I was in complete control—but of what? I wondered. What do all these switches do?

I peered closely at the switches.

I searched for writing underneath them—some sign of what they did.

Nothing.

Well, there was only one way to find out!

My fingertips tingled with anticipation.

Santa's beard? Kid stuff!

Merry Christmas, everyone, I thought with glee. Get ready for some *real* excitement!

I slowly reached out my hand—to a big red switch in the middle of the control board.

I grasped it between my fingertips.

And flipped it.

I waited.

And waited.

And listened to the shoppers' voices outside the

door. Listened for their shrieks—as the lights went out. Or the sprinkler system went on. Something.

No cries of surprise.

Nothing.

I sighed and flipped a big blue switch right next to the red one.

Bam!

I jumped.

The door locked—with the sound of a heavy bolt.

I flipped the blue switch again. I listened for the bolt to slide open. It didn't. I was trapped!

3

I grabbed the doorknob and turned it. The door remained locked.

I jiggled the knob.

Tugged on the door again.

It didn't budge.

It was bolted shut—from the outside.

A small wave of panic rose up inside me.

I stared around the room.

The lights seemed to blink more wildly. The humming sound seemed to grow louder.

Relax, Kenny, I told myself. If you bang on the door, somebody will hear you and let you out.

I listened.

I heard only the low hum of the control panels.

"Hey, could someone open this door?" I shouted. "I'm stuck in here."

No one answered me.

"Hey, I'm stuck in here!" I yelled, pounding my fist on the door. "Somebody open up!"

No one came to the door.

With all the people out there, why didn't anyone hear me?

"I'm a kid trapped in this closet!" I yelled as loud as I could. "Help me! Somebody! Get me out of here!"

I banged on the door with my hands. I kicked it hard with my feet.

There! Somebody had to hear that!

Silence.

An uneasy feeling crept into the pit of my stomach. I stood back from the door and took a deep breath.

Then I took a running leap at it, throwing my shoulder against it hard.

Nothing.

I banged on the door until my knuckles hurt.

Still nothing.

Where is everyone?

I glanced at my glow-in-the-dark watch: 8:15!

Dalby's closes at eight.

Did everyone go home?

How could that be?

How could everyone have gone home and left me in here? My mom must have told someone I was missing. Why weren't they looking for me?

My hands began to sweat. I had to get out of this place. But how?

I wiped my sweaty palms on my pants and checked my watch again: 8:20.

It wasn't that late. There had to be someone in the store. A manager. A security guard locking up. One of Santa's stupid elves. Someone.

Oh, I get it! They know I'm in here, I realized. They're trying to teach me a lesson or something dumb like that.

"Come on, you guys!" I yelled. "Please. Let me out of here! Now!"

No reply.

I grabbed the doorknob and pulled with all my strength.

"Help!" I screamed. "Help!"

I twisted the knob. Then I pulled again, as hard as I could.

"Let me out of here!" I shouted.

No one answered my calls. I backed away from the door, wondering what to do next.

That's when I heard the sizzling sounds.

I gazed around the room. I couldn't tell what was making that noise.

Then, suddenly, the hum in the room grew louder.

And the floor began to vibrate.

My legs shook hard.

The humming grew louder. Louder. It filled the room now, shrill and strong. It seemed to come at me from every direction, all at once.

The floor quaked under my feet.

I started to lose my balance.

Started to slam into the control panel—when the door slowly swung open.

4

I grabbed onto the control panel and caught my balance.

I stared at the door.

It swung open some more. A pale red light glowed through the opening.

I staggered toward the door on shaky legs.

"What took you so long?" I demanded as I stepped outside. "Something crazy was going on in that room!"

Huh?

No one stood outside the door.

The toy department sat in silence. Except for

the dull red glow from the exit signs, it was totally dark.

As my eyes adjusted to the dim light, I glanced around. In the shadowy light, I could make out the outline of Santa's Village.

In the glow of the red light, Santa Street looked eerie—like a miniature Fear Street. The deserted end of Fear Street. The part with the abandoned mansions. The mansions that people say are haunted.

I live on Fear Street. I have to admit it—the mansions do look kind of creepy. But haunted— come on! How could anyone really believe in ghosts?

I took a step forward.

"Hey!" I shouted. "Anybody here?"

My voice echoed back to me.

I took a few more steps. My sneakers squeaked on the marble floor.

I stood perfectly still and listened. All I heard was my own heart beating. Really loud.

Then I heard something else.

I held my breath. What was it?

It sounded like—bells.

Sleigh bells. Louder now. Coming closer—from Santa's Village.

I took a few steps through the village gate.

"Hey, is someone there?" I yelled.

Footsteps. Slow and heavy.

I squinted in the darkness. I saw something move—down by Santa's sleigh.

I could make out a shadow now—the shadow of a man. A man sitting in Santa's sleigh.

He stood up and stepped out of the sleigh.

Even in the shadows I could tell he was big. And tall. He walked slowly down Santa Street—right toward me.

"Who's there?" I shouted. "Who is it?" My voice squeaked a little.

The man didn't answer.

He came closer.

I heard his heavy shoes scrape the floor.

And with every step he took, I heard the faint sound of jingling bells.

Barely breathing, I stood there and watched him. Now I could make out his fur-trimmed red coat and red pants.

Joe!

Joe—still wearing his big white beard. Didn't he ever take that thing off?

"Hey, did you unlock that door for me?" I called out to him.

He shrugged. "Maybe I did. Maybe I didn't."

"Give me a break, Joe." I rolled my eyes at him. "It sure took you long enough," I complained. "I yelled my head off in there. Didn't you hear me?"

"I'm a busy guy tonight," Joe replied. "Tonight's the big night."

"All right. All right. You're still mad at me for pulling your beard off," I said sarcastically. "You wanted to teach me a lesson, right?"

Joe walked up to me and stared down into my eyes. He shook his head slowly from side to side. I noticed a funny little smile under his beard.

"Are you sorry about what you did, Kenny?" he asked.

"What's the big deal?" I scoffed. "Those kids will get over it."

"You've been naughty all year, Kenny," Joe said grimly.

"Naughty?" I mimicked his voice. Then I chuckled. "You can save the Santa act for next year. Okay, Joe?"

Joe wagged his finger, frowning.

"Come on, Joe. Lighten up," I teased. "You don't have to drag out this Santa act for me."

Then I reached up. I grabbed hold of his beard—and gave it a good yank.

It didn't budge.

I pulled on it again—harder this time.

It didn't come off.

With a shaky hand, I reached out to give it a really hard tug.

5

"**W**-what did you stick this thing on with anyway?" I stammered.

Joe's round cheeks puffed out. They turned really red.

He gripped my hand strongly. He pried it off his beard. But he didn't let go of my wrist.

I stared up into his face—and studied it closely. Even in the shadowy light this guy didn't look that much like Joe to me anymore.

My mouth suddenly felt very dry. I licked my lips and tugged my wrist out of his hand.

I took a quick step backward. Away from him. Whoever he was . . .

"That beard. It's—it's real, right?" I murmured.

"That's right." He nodded slowly. A small bell on his cap jingled. It sounded creepy in the silent department store.

"And you're not Joe," I blurted out.

"Right again." He crossed his arms over his wide chest. "It's time we had a talk, Kenny," the stranger said to me. His deep voice boomed through the empty store.

He moved even closer.

"Talk? About what?" I asked slowly.

"About you, Kenny," he said.

"What do you mean, about me? Who are you anyway?" I shot back.

"Ho-ho-ho!" he laughed. The sound came from deep in his belly. His entire body shook. "You're kidding me, Kenny. Right?"

"I'm not kidding," I shouted at him. "How am I supposed to know who you are? You stomp around here, dressed in that stupid Santa suit. Trying to scare me, or something—"

"Are you sure you don't know me, Kenny?" He leaned over, his face very close to mine. "You're a smart kid. Think about it."

I stared up at him.

I thought about it.

Only one answer made sense.

No. Impossible.

"Well?" he asked.

"This is a joke, right?" I answered. "Pretty good." I forced a laugh. "You really had me going there for a minute. Well, see you around. My folks must be looking for me. They must be worried."

"You can't go yet, Kenny." The big man shook his head. "Not until we've had our talk."

"Hey, I'm sorry about the beard," I said in a rush. "It was just a little joke. I'm really sorry, honest."

"You've got a lot more than the beard to apologize for," he replied in that booming voice. "You've done a lot of bad things. It's time for you to learn—before it's too late."

"Come along," he ordered me. He grabbed my sleeve and led me to the ballerina-doll display.

He reached down and pulled out a doll from the bottom of the pile. The ballerina doll Kristi had shown me.

The doll's hair was totally flattened. Her eyes, permanently jammed shut.

"Did you do this?" he asked me.

"I was just teasing Kristi a little. No big deal," I said. "It's not as though I hurt anyone for real. The doll can't feel anything."

"But little girls can," he said, gently lifting the doll's lids. "And so can classmates. And parents. And school custodians."

He set the doll carefully back on the display. Then he turned to me.

"So, is that it? Is that what you wanted to show me?" I asked eagerly. "I really have to go now. It's really getting late."

I turned to make a run for it. I waved at him over my shoulder.

"See you!" I called out.

"Not so fast." He reached out and grabbed my arm. He stared deeply into my eyes.

I tried to squirm out of his hold, but I couldn't.

"By tomorrow morning you will be a different boy, Kenny. A nice, decent kid. Kind and thoughtful. Considerate of other people's feelings. You won't think it's fun anymore to play mean tricks. Or hurt people's feelings. What do think of that?"

"Great," I said nervously. "Can I go now?"

"No, Kenny. Some friends of mine are coming to visit you," he told me. His voice sounded serious. Real serious.

Not a good sign.

"Friends?" I croaked. "Why do your friends want to see me?"

27

"You'll find out," he said. "The first will come at nine o'clock. The second, at ten. And the third one, at the stroke of midnight."

"Midnight," I repeated. "Gee, I'm sorry, but I can't stay till midnight." I wrestled free of his grip and started to walk away.

Is he going to try to stop me?

No.

He just stood there and watched me go.

I breathed a long sigh of relief.

I headed for the escalator. It wasn't moving. I ran all the way down it to the main floor.

The aisle straight ahead of me glowed with the red light of the exit sign. I headed toward the sign.

But when I reached it, I couldn't find the door.

No door in sight.

Far off, on the other side of the store, I spotted another glowing exit sign.

I charged across the main aisle—past the shadowy shapes of handbags, perfumes, and ladies' hats—straight for the sign.

Hey! What's going on here!

Under the exit sign I found a solid wall.

No door.

I ran through the shoe department. To the back of the store. To another exit sign.

No door!

I heard footsteps. Heavy footsteps. And the faint jingling of bells.

I spun around and faced the bearded stranger again. "Hey, how am I supposed to get out of here?"

"You're not leaving, Kenny. Not tonight," he told me in a calm, quiet tone.

But I felt a chill.

"I can't stay here all night," I protested. "You can't leave me here all alone."

He placed his heavy hand on my shoulder. He wore black leather gloves now. And beside him, I spotted a huge red sack—so stuffed, it looked about to burst.

"You won't be alone, Kenny," he reminded me. "My friends are going to visit you. You're going to have a Christmas Eve you'll never forget."

I didn't like the sound of that one bit.

My throat suddenly felt tight.

"Who—who are your friends?" I murmured.

"Ghosts, Kenny," the bearded man replied. His eyes twinkled in the darkness. "Three ghosts who love to have fun. And play jokes. Just like you."

He leaned over and hoisted the huge sack to his shoulder. Then he started to walk away.

"Merry Christmas, Kenny." As he gave a short wave, his figure grew fainter and fainter.

He was disappearing—right before my eyes!

"Wait!" I called out to him.

"Remember, the first at nine o'clock. The second at ten—"

I jumped forward and tried to grab him.

But he was a shadow now. A dim shadow—fading fast.

"And the third at the stroke of midnight."

His words hung in the air.

And before they'd died away, he was gone!

6

"**H**ey!" I called out. "Come back!"

I spun around. I searched the shadows.

"Where are you?" I shouted.

My voice echoed all around me.

Ghosts, Kenny. Three ghosts who love to have fun. And play jokes. Just like you. His words came back to me.

Ghosts. Give me a break.

Did he really think I was going believe that one?

I checked my watch.

Ten minutes to nine.

The first ghost was supposed to show up at nine.

I felt my heartbeat quicken. Then I laughed at myself.

Get a grip, Kenny, I told myself. Do you really think a ghost is going to appear in ten minutes? In the middle of Dalby's Department Store?

Yeah, right.

I gazed around the darkened store, searching for another exit sign. I spotted one over in a corner of the store and jogged to it.

As I brushed past the scarves, I felt someone watching me. The bearded man. Hiding somewhere in the shadows.

I could feel his eyes on me.

I stopped and spun around.

"Hey, I know you're there," I shouted into the darkness. "Come on. Show me the way out of here."

No reply.

"Oh, forget it. I'll find my own way out of here," I muttered.

I continued toward the exit sign. The rubber soles of my sneakers slapped against the marble floor, echoing in the darkness.

I came to the end of the aisle.

To another exit sign.

Another exit sign with no door underneath it!

What's going on here?

I kicked the spot on the wall where the door should have been.

How could all the doors just disappear? This didn't make any sense!

A cold bead of sweat trickled down the middle of my forehead.

I spun around. I turned down the next aisle.

The red glow of the exit sign reflected off the glass counters. Counters stacked with lipsticks, makeup, and perfume bottles.

I searched frantically for a door. There had to be one somewhere.

I walked down another aisle. And another.

I jogged by dummies. Rows of dummies wearing gloves.

Dummies with outstretched arms.

Dummies reaching over the counters. Reaching into the aisles with their black-gloved hands.

Stretching forward. Reaching out for me.

My heart pounded in my chest.

They're just dummies. They can't move.

I broke into a run.

And stopped short.

Something snagged my jacket. Yanked me backward.

I peered down—and gasped.

33

7

A hand gripped my jacket.

The black-gloved hand of a dummy.

I yanked my arm free.

You ran into it. You ran into the dummy—and it snagged you, I convinced myself.

I started to run again.

I glanced down to check my watch—five minutes to nine.

My pulse began to race.

What should I do? I can't find a door anywhere in this whole store. Where should I go?

A telephone.

That's it! I'll use the pay phone on the second

floor to call home. I know just where it is, too. I used it last week to call Dad to pick me up.

I raced to the escalator and took the metal steps two at a time. I ran down a long aisle of kitchen appliances—blenders, toasters, microwave ovens—and saw someone standing at the end of the aisle.

A tall, thin man.

Yes! Someone to help me.

"Hey!" I yelled as I ran toward him. "I'm stuck in here. I can't find the doors downstairs—"

The man stood frozen.

Didn't he hear me?

I ran up to him so fast—I knocked him over.

I felt like a total jerk.

I'd been yelling at a big cardboard figure. The figure of Tex Tabasco—a famous chef with his own TV show—holding up a frying pan that was on sale.

I got so mad, I jumped on Tex. Stomped on him hard. That's when I saw the blue-and-white sign glowing in the distance: TELEPHONE.

I left Tex crumpled on the floor and charged through the bedding department—past rows of beds covered with thick, fluffy quilts.

My sneakers screeched to a halt.

Under the sign for the telephone, there was—nothing.

No phone under the sign.

No phone anywhere.

"I don't get it!" I screamed. *"What is going on around here?"*

I sat down on a bed next to me. "Think, Kenny," I ordered myself. "Something crazy is going on here. You have to find a way out. *Now!*"

I thought hard. And yawned.

Suddenly, I felt so tired.

My eyelids felt heavy. They began to close.

I forced them open.

"You can't sleep now! What's wrong with you?" I yelled at myself. *"You have to get out of here!"*

I leaned back against the soft pillow on the bed. Snuggled under the fluffy quilt.

"Get up!" I ordered myself.

But I couldn't. I don't know why. I just couldn't. My body felt so heavy. So tired suddenly.

I glanced at my watch: 8:59.

"I've got to get out of here," I mumbled.

My eyes closed. For a minute? For an hour? I didn't know.

A loud bang jolted me out of my sleep.

My eyelids flew open.

The bed's big brass headboard vibrated. Banged against the wall.

Faster and faster.

The entire bed quaked.

I tried to sit up. But the bed shook so hard, I couldn't keep my balance.

Something white and powdery showered down on my face. I brushed it off and glanced up.

The chandelier above the bed swung wildly. Tiny bits of the ceiling snowed down on me.

What was happening? Was it an earthquake? In Shadyside?

The entire bedding department shook now. The beds bounced up and down. Their legs pounded the floor. China lamps crashed all around me.

And then I heard a roar that echoed through the dark store. The roar of a huge, powerful engine.

The roar grew louder.

Coming from everywhere at once.

I gripped the shaking bed. Struggled to sit up.

I stared into the blackness. The sound was almost deafening. Coming closer.

Something flashed in the dark. What was it? A beam of light? A flashing beam of light?

Where did it come from?

It disappeared as quickly as it had appeared.

Then it flashed again. This time directly into my eyes!

I shielded my eyes with my hand.
"Who's there?" I screamed.
And then I saw it—a big, gleaming motorcycle.
Charging down the aisle.
Coming straight at me!

8

"Turn! Turn!" I screamed.

The headlight blinded me as the motorcycle headed straight for me.

I gripped the bed, frozen with fear.

I closed my eyes—and waited for the crash.

But it didn't come.

I heard the squeal of brakes and breathed in the smell of burning rubber.

I peered up from the bed—and saw the giant front wheel, spinning in midair. Inches from my head.

The headlight lit up the ceiling above me.

I looked at the driver—and my whole body shuddered.

The driver wore a big silver helmet, his eyes masked by a deep black visor. The rest of his face was covered by a bristly black beard.

His body was huge. He wore a black T-shirt and a black vest. But it was the chains that made me gasp—big, heavy chains draped over his shoulders, crossing his chest. And tied around his waist.

His muscular arms held the bike up—with the front wheel spinning. Spinning right next to my face.

I opened my mouth to speak, but no words came out.

The biker stared at me.

He gunned the thundering engine—and I leaped back. Then he lowered the bike, slamming the front wheel on the floor.

I swallowed hard. I held my breath.

The motor's roar died.

The biker's lips slowly parted into a grin. A mouthful of metal teeth glistened in the darkness.

"Hi, Kenny!" he growled. "Ready to have some fun?"

9

"**H**-how do you know my name?" I stammered.

He laughed at me. A laugh that boomed like thunder.

I wiped my sweaty hands on my jacket and slid out of the bed. I took a good look at him.

He leaned against his bike now, arms crossed over his barrel-sized chest.

His massive shoulders bulged beneath his T-shirt. On his wrists, thick leather bands glistened with pointed silver studs.

The huge chains—with links bigger than my fist—snaked across his body.

Then I saw his skin. His blue skin.

No. Not blue, I realized. Tattoos. Every inch of his skin, covered with them.

My eyes followed a thick blue-and-green tattoo of a snake that swirled up his arm to his bulging bicep. The snake's beady red eyes seemed to glare at me.

And then I saw its red tongue flicker—and I screamed.

The biker chuckled—as the snake let out a low hiss.

I watched in horror as the snake's thick blue tail slithered around the biker's wrist.

I sucked in a breath.

"Like the tattoos?" the biker asked.

"Yeah, really cool," I choked out.

Then I gasped—as a big black spider suddenly came alive. It twitched on the biker's forearm—and scampered up to his elbow. Then it disappeared beneath his T-shirt sleeve.

Just below the edge of his sleeve, a purple skull with glowing yellow eyes winked at me.

I gulped and looked away.

"Wh-who are you?" I stammered.

"They call me Night Watchman," he grumbled.

"S-so you watch the store?" I asked nervously.

"Wrong, kid." The Night Watchman slowly shook his head. "I've been watching *you.*"

His reply sent an icy chill down my back.

"What do you think you're doing in here?" he demanded.

"I—I got locked up in here. It wasn't my fault. Honest," I sputtered. "See, I got stuck in the computer control room. And then—"

The biker swung a massive leg over his bike as I spoke. He settled into the seat, grabbed the long, curvy handlebars, and adjusted the hand gear. Then he raised his right boot and slammed it down on the pedal.

Long blue flames exploded out of the silver tailpipes. I leaped to the side to stand clear.

Great, he's leaving! I thought.

"Get on!" he yelled. His voice bellowed over the engine's roar.

"That's okay." I waved at him. "I can find my own way out."

He pointed to the space behind him on the bike's saddle. *"Now!"* he commanded.

He glared at me. His thin lips curled into a snarl.

Shaking, I stepped up to the bike and jumped on the back.

I searched for something to hold on to. Anything but the Night Watchman himself.

The bike engine roared and surged forward.

Whoa! My head snapped back as we blasted off.

I threw my arms around the Night Watchman's waist.

I gasped.

My arms passed right through him.

I could still see his wide, leather-covered back. I could still see the chains winding around his body. But I couldn't feel a thing.

Nothing.

The Night Watchman was a ghost.

10

A ghost!

I gripped the seat—until the bike slowed. Until I could leap off.

But the biker zoomed through the aisles of the bedding department—faster and faster.

I gathered up my courage to speak. "Slow down!" I begged.

"Faster?" he replied. "You want to go faster? No problem!"

He revved the engine higher. Then he tossed back his head and bellowed a ghostly laugh. "Ha-ha-ha!"

"Let me off!" I screamed.

"Stop! Let me off!" I released one hand from the seat and pounded on his back.

My fist passed right through him—striking the air.

"Having fun back there, Kenny?" the Night Watchman yelled over his shoulder.

We sped through the china department—and hit the first set of shelves, head-on.

CRASHHHH!

Smashed dishes flew everywhere. I lowered my head, trying to shield my face from the pieces of china that rained down on us.

"Let me off!" I screamed again and again.

The Night Watchman threw back his head and laughed. "Hey, where's your sense of humor, kid? I thought you loved a good joke. Don't tell me you didn't like that?"

"No-o-o," I stammered. "Enough. Let me off!"

"Off?" he said. "No problem. Just as soon as we get to the third floor."

The third floor?

I peeked over his shoulder—and gasped.

Straight ahead. The escalator to the third floor.

He wasn't going to drive a motorcycle up an escalator—was he?

WHAMMMM!

The front wheel slammed up the first step. And the next and the next.

My body rattled as we climbed up and up.

I closed my eyes tightly—and held my breath.

We reached the third floor.

I let out a long whoosh of air.

Then I inhaled sharply as we took a sudden turn—and headed for the electronics department.

The Night Watchman slowed the bike now—slow enough for me to escape.

As he turned down the television aisle, I leaped off.

Yes! Safe at last! Now I'll escape. Find a way out of here, I told myself. The worst part is over.

I didn't know how wrong I was.

SQUEEEAAAAAL!

The Night Watchman hit the brakes. The bike skidded to a stop.

"Come here, kid!" he boomed.

I turned and ran.

I headed for the escalator—and felt a force pulling me back. Back down the aisle. Back toward the TVs. Back to the Night Watchman.

"Going someplace, Kenny?"

"I have to get home," I groaned.

"And miss the entertainment?" he sneered.

Entertainment?

What was he talking about? I didn't want to find out.

I spun around—and bolted for the escalator.

And slammed straight into the Night Watchman. This time, his body felt like a brick wall.

I flew backward and landed on the floor.

"Don't waste my time," he growled. "You can't escape me. I'm a ghost—remember? I am the ghost of your past."

"Wh-what does that mean?" I stammered.

"I'm disappointed in you, Kenny." The Night Watchman folded his arms across his chest. "Haven't you figured it out yet?"

"Figured what out?" I glanced up at him. "I don't know what you're talking about!"

"Let me spell it out for you, kid. I am the Ghost of Christmas Past. *Your* past," he declared.

He grabbed the back of my jacket and lifted me off my feet. The heels of his black boots clicked on the hard floor as he pulled me into the video department.

"Sit!" He shoved me down. I hit the floor with a thud.

Then he began searching through a stack of videos.

"I can watch a movie at home!" I exclaimed. "I have to get home!"

49

"Sorry, Kenny," he said. "You don't have *this* movie at your house."

He inserted the tape into a VCR.

The screen on a giant TV lit up. I saw a street. A familiar street.

"Hey, that's Main Street!" I said. "I never knew they made a movie in Shadyside!"

The Night Watchman leaned against his bike. He took a long, pointy metal toothpick from the pocket of his T-shirt and slipped it between his teeth.

"This is going to be a real treat for you, Kenny!" he sneered as he picked at his metal teeth.

I turned back to the screen. The camera panned down street after street—filled with people, bundled up in their winter coats. They carried shopping bags and boxes and wrapped packages. Christmas presents!

"Hey, someone must have shot this video today," I said.

"Hmmm." The Night Watchman shook his head from side to side. "Keep watching, Kenny."

The camera zoomed in on a building—my school!

Then the auditorium flashed on the TV screen. The principal stood on the stage, in front of a microphone.

"Students of Shadyside Middle School," his voice boomed. "I hope you all enjoyed the Christmas show."

"Hey! Wait a minute. What's going on?" I said. "Our drama teacher broke her leg this Thanksgiving. So we didn't put on a Christmas play this year."

I shot a glance at the Night Watchman. "Keep watching, Kenny."

"Now, here to make our annual Christmas speech, is one of the nicest boys in our school," the principal went on. "Timmy Smathers!"

The camera zoomed in on nerdy Tiny Timmy. He sat in the first row.

I stared hard at the screen. This all looked so familiar, as if I'd seen it before.

All the kids clapped and Timmy stood up. Shuffling sheets and sheets of paper in his hands, he walked up the stage steps toward the podium.

Then—from the back of the stage—a figure inched forward in the shadows. I didn't know who it was at first. I couldn't see his face.

Then it hit me!

I knew what I was watching.

"Hey, that's me!" I exclaimed.

"Do you remember what you did there?" the Night Watchman asked.

"How could I forget?" I declared. "It was last Christmas." Just the memory of that day made me laugh.

I turned back to the screen—just in time to see me duck behind the podium.

I picked up the special stand the woodworking shop had made just for Timmy. He needed a stool to stand on because he was so short!

I watched me run off the stage, clutching the stand to my chest. Timmy walked up to the podium and rested the pages of his speech on top.

"Fellow students of Shadyside Middle School," he began. "At this special time of year, we all . . ."

Timmy waved his hands in the air as he spoke. And that's all we could see of him—his hands, waving in the air. The rest of him was hidden behind the podium.

The camera panned over the audience. At first, only a few kids laughed. You could hear some other kids shushing them.

Then the laughter grew louder. Finally, even the shushers were giggling!

It was a riot!

The camera zoomed in on me. I sat in the last row. I started to chant.

"Ti-ny Tim-my! Ti-ny Tim-my!" It didn't take long for the other kids to join in.

The camera zoomed back to the stage. Behind the podium, Timmy bit his lip. A tear streamed down his face.

The principal stormed onto the stage.

The Night Watchman slammed his hand on Stop. Timmy froze on the screen, his face wet with tears.

"Had enough?" he asked.

"Why did you stop it?" I exclaimed. "This is where it gets really good."

"Because *I've* had enough," the Night Watchman said.

He pounded his fist on the top of the VCR. The VCR crumpled. The tape spewed out.

Then he flipped up his dark visor—and I saw his eyes.

Creepy yellow eyes with no eyelids. No eyelashes.

My whole body trembled.

"Nowww—what do you think?" he crooned.

I stared in terror as his yellow eyes began to glow.

"Still think I'm crazy, Kenny?"

I broke out into a sweat.

I tried to speak, but the words stuck in my throat.

"Timmy didn't forget that little prank you pulled

last Christmas," the ghost roared. "What you did hurt him, Kenny."

"T-take it easy," I finally choked out. "Th-that's Timmy's problem. Not mine."

The ghost shook his head. "That's where you're wrong. It's *your* problem, Kenny!"

12

The Night Watchman's thin lips curled into a smile. A horrible, ghostly smile.

He stepped toward me—his thick fingers clenched into two tight fists.

Run! I told myself. *Get up and run!*

But I couldn't move.

"It—it was a joke," I stammered. "It was just a prank!"

"You're going to pay for what you did to Timmy," he shouted. His big hands reached out to grab me. I ducked.

I jumped up from the floor and ran.

My heart pounded against my ribs.

I dashed past the long row of TVs. Behind me, I heard the bike's engine thunder to life.

I skidded around the first corner I came to. I saw the furniture department ahead of me. Chairs . . . couches . . . tables. Separated with little walls. Little, fake rooms.

There had to be someplace for me to hide in there!

The bike roared closer.

I dashed through the rooms. In and out. Zig-zagging in circles.

Wherever I turned, I heard the bike right behind me.

"You can't escape, Kenny," the ghost bellowed. "Give up!"

My sides ached from running.

I heard the bike crash through a table as it followed my trail.

"I'm coming for you, Kenny!" the ghost shrieked. Even over the engine I could hear his wicked laughter—and the heavy chains he wore, rattling and clanging.

"Hide-and-seek is over, Kenny," he cackled madly now. "You lose!"

I ran out of the furniture department.

The bike engine roared through the store, echoing all round me.

I ran and ran—right to the railing straight ahead of me.

I peered over it.

I could see the second floor down below—the home workshop department.

The power saw display. With its rows and rows of knife-sharp edges glistening up at me.

"Time to get my point, Kenny! Good joke, right?"

I spun around.

The ghost sat on his bike—only a few feet in front of me. He had appeared quietly. Out of nowhere!

"Can't we talk about this?" I gulped.

The ghost revved his engine in reply.

My eyes darted nervously to the left. Then to the right. I was trapped—nowhere to run.

I peered down to the second floor. At the razor-sharp blades lined up directly beneath me.

I glanced back at the ghost. His eyes glowed in the dark—a deep yellow glow.

My heart raced. The veins pulsated in my neck.

The ghost flipped his black visor down. Tightened the straps on his helmet.

"Happy landings, Kenny," he roared. His face broke out in a wide, evil smile.

Then he turned up the throttle on his bike—and headed straight for me.

I squeezed my eyes closed.

"Nooooo!" I shrieked as I leaped over the railing.

And plunged down.

Down.

Down to the razor-sharp blades below.

13

I landed with a heavy thud.

I was afraid to open my eyes.

Afraid to move. Afraid to feel the pointed blades cutting through my skin.

But nothing hurt. I didn't feel anything sharp.

In fact, whatever was beneath me felt—soft.

I opened my eyes—and gasped.

I was lying in a bed!

I sat up and gazed around me. Yes. I was back in the bedding department. Back in the same bed!

What happened to the Night Watchman? I sat up, tense and alert. My heart began to pound. I listened for the motorcycle.

Nothing.

The store stood dark and silent.

Did I dream the whole thing? Did I fall asleep and have a horrible nightmare?

Maybe. Probably, I told myself. After all, no one rides through Dalby's on a motorcycle.

And there are no such things as ghosts!

My heart began to slow down. I was starting to feel a little better.

I glanced at my watch.

Almost ten P.M.

Then I remembered what Santa said. The first ghost at nine. The second ghost at ten.

I shivered and pulled the comforter up around my shoulders.

"There are no such thing as ghosts," I told myself again.

I slipped my feet over the edge of the bed.

Time to search for a way out of here. I yawned.

I felt so sleepy again. And cold. Chilled to the bone. I shivered and lifted my legs back onto the mattress.

I pulled the quilt up to my chin. Did they have to turn the heat off at night? I yawned loudly as my head hit the pillow.

So sleepy.

So cold.

I pulled my knees up to my chest and wrapped the comforter snugly around me.

The room grew icy.

I shivered hard. My teeth chattered.

I wished I were home. Where was Mom? Why didn't she wait for me?

A gust of wind suddenly blew through the store. Across the aisle, a display of curtains flapped and swirled in its wake.

The wind howled through the aisles. Blowing stronger.

Hey, there aren't any windows in Dalby's! Where was that wind coming from?

A freezing blast of air stung my face and eyes. I trembled—huddled in a frozen ball on the bed.

The wind tore at my quilt. It snapped and billowed in the powerful gusts. I clung on to it desperately.

The wind rose again, raging now—ripping the quilt from my grasp. It soared to the ceiling on a current of air.

Rows of curtains ripped from their rods. Towels and bath mats flew from the shelves.

Another blast of air whipped through the store, hurling a metal curtain rod right at me.

I lifted my pillow to block it. The rod bounced off the pillow and crashed to the floor.

But the wind beat against my pillow—and tore it wide open.

I grabbed for another pillow. But all the pillows on all the beds were sailing through the air now. The wind beat at them—tearing them to shreds. Feathers and foam swirled everywhere.

Feathers and foam swirling, swirling—then drifting down on me. Cold and wet.

Cold and wet!

The feathers had turned to snow.

Snow? In the middle of Dalby's?

"Night Watchman?" I shouted, my words swallowed by the freezing wind. "Are you out there? Are you doing this to me?"

I spotted something coming toward me.

No—not something.

Someone.

In a long, swirling robe. White as the snowflakes that whirled overhead.

Icicles hung from his face. Glistening icicles—dripping down from his white hair and his long, stringy beard.

He glided slowly toward me through the swirling snow.

My pulse quickened.

As he came closer, I could make out his ghastly

face. A face carved out of a rough chunk of ice—
with cold blue eyes trapped inside its glassy walls.

And frosty, hollowed cheeks.

And a long, jagged cut for a mouth.

"Ken-ny," he wailed in a voice like the freezing,
howling wind.

"Who . . . are . . . you?" I screamed. "What . . .
are . . . you?"

He moved closer. An icy, clawed hand slipped out
from the long sleeve of his robe. It glistened in the
darkness.

I inched back on the bed. As far back as I could
go.

The robed creature reached out—and clamped
his frozen hand on my shoulder.

An icy blast shot through my veins.

"Kenny," the creature groaned. "I am your
Christmas Present!"

14

The creature squeezed my shoulder hard and another chill surged through my veins.

"Who—who are you?" I asked again, my teeth chattering.

"I am called the Iceman," he declared.

I tried to pull away, but he tightened his grip.

Snow fell harder. Icy flakes stung my face.

The frigid wind stormed through the store.

"I'm f-freezing!" My teeth chattered. "Make it stop!"

A gruesome smile twisted the Iceman's lips. "You get used to it," he said, "after a while."

"But you're a ghost!" I exclaimed.

"You'll get used to that too!" he rasped.

I gulped back a huge lump in my throat.

Was I going to freeze to death—and turn into a ghost too?

No way, I shuddered, shaking my head.

I felt something strange clinging to my hair.

I reached up and touched it.

A long icicle.

Oh, no!

"What are you doing to me?" I cried.

"Nothing yet," he replied in a low voice. "Now—look up."

I glanced up—and saw the sky! The stars and moon were fading. The sun was beginning to rise.

When I glanced back down, Dalby's had disappeared.

Totally vanished.

We were standing outside!

Yes! I had finally escaped Dalby's!

"Where are we?" I asked with excitement.

"Don't you recognize Fear Street?" the Iceman groaned.

I spun around and saw my own house. We stood on the sidewalk, right out front. A Christmas wreath hung on our front door. A wave of happiness and relief washed over me.

"Is it Christmas morning already?" I asked eagerly. "Everything is okay now, isn't it?"

The Iceman shook his head again. "For you, it is your darkest hour," he announced.

"But it's Christmas! And I'm home!" I exclaimed.

The Iceman glanced at our picket gate. A sharp gust of wind blew it open. He pointed an icy finger at me.

"Go!" he commanded.

I walked up our path.

The Iceman floated behind me.

I still felt really cold. Chilled to the bone.

I hugged my body and rubbed my arms.

I'll warm up when I get inside, I told myself.

I reached the front door and peeked through the living room window. Sure enough, Mom, Dad, and Kristi sat around the fireplace. Decorated for Christmas, our tree stood off to the side, twinkling with bright, colorful lights.

I sighed.

It was Christmas—and I was home.

I reached for the bell on the front door.

The Iceman's frozen fingers brushed my hand aside. "Why disturb them?" he asked.

"We keep the door locked," I explained. "And I don't have a key."

66

"You're a smart boy, Kenny," the Iceman declared. "Haven't you figured out that we don't need a key?"

"Huh?"

He didn't wait to explain. He took a step—and his foot went right through the door!

"Come on, Kenny!"

"I can't!" I said.

The Iceman's frozen hand locked around my wrist. He jerked me forward.

Oh, no! I closed my eyes, ready to smack into the door.

But I didn't.

My body floated right through it!

I gazed down and checked myself out.

How did this happen?

"But *I'm* not a ghost!" I exclaimed as I stood in our front hall.

"Not yet," the Iceman replied with a shrug. He gestured to the living room.

Mom, Dad, and Kristi sat beside the fire. I expected to see them opening their presents. But I spotted the gifts piled neatly under the tree. Still wrapped.

Weird.

"He's gone," Kristi sobbed. "He's gone and he's never coming back!"

"Sometimes these things happen," Mom comforted her. She patted Kristi tenderly on the shoulder.

"But it's not fair!" Kristi cried. "I miss him so much!"

My father rose and picked up the biggest box under the tree. "Here, honey," he urged Kristi. "Open it. It will cheer you up!"

"Nothing is going to cheer me up," Kristi replied tearfully. "Not till he's home, safe and sound."

I saw Mom and Dad exchange sad looks.

I didn't have to ask why. They missed me!

I couldn't stand seeing them so miserable.

I pulled away from the Iceman and ran toward them. "I'm home, Mom and Dad!" I yelled. "I'm home, Kristi! Everything is okay. We can all celebrate Christmas together."

But no one looked up.

Didn't they see me?

"I'm right here," I shouted. "Please don't cry anymore. I'm back!"

But Kristi kept crying.

Mom and Dad looked grim.

I turned back to the Iceman. "What's wrong with them?" I asked.

The Iceman shrugged. "They can't see you,

Kenny," he grumbled. "They can't hear you either."

"Why not?" I asked. "What's wrong?"

The doorbell rang. My dad went to answer it.

Timmy Smathers stood on the front steps.

Oh, great! What did that geek want now?

"Merry Christmas, Mr. Frobisher!" he exclaimed.

"I'm afraid it's not very merry for us," my father announced gloomily. "Not this year."

Pushing back the hood on his parka, Timmy stepped into the hall. I noticed a leash in his hand. As Timmy tugged on it, a dog bounded to the middle of the living room!

Rags! Our cocker spaniel.

Why did Timmy have Rags?

"Woof! Woof!" Rags barked, and jumped around, wagging his tail.

"Rags!" Kristi squealed. "You did come back. You're home! You're home—safe and sound!"

She kneeled down and Rags jumped into her arms. He licked her all over the face. Mom stepped over and patted Rags on the head.

"I guess things really do work out for the best, don't they?" Mom sighed happily.

"Well, it wouldn't be Christmas without Rags!" Dad declared.

I bit back a startled cry.

They hadn't missed me!

All those tears had been for Rags! Our dog!

"Thank you, Timmy." Dad clapped Timmy on the back. "Thanks for finding Rags and bringing him home. Now we can really have a Merry Christmas!"

"Please, Timmy. Why don't you stay and have something to eat with us?" Mom suggested.

Timmy glanced at the dining room table, all set for Christmas dinner.

"Gee, your dinner looks delicious. And we ate ours really early," he replied. "Just looking at that delicious food—makes me feel hungry all over again.

"Then it's settled!" Mom exclaimed. "You'll stay for dinner."

"Are you sure?" Timmy asked. "I mean, do you have enough?

"Sure, Timmy! You can take Kenny's portion," Dad said cheerfully.

"You can't do that, Dad!" I burst out. "What about me? What am I going to eat?"

But I'd forgotten.

Dad couldn't see me. Or hear a word I said.

"Kenny's never on time for dinner anyway," he explained to Timmy. "Even on Christmas!"

"I don't believe it!" I groaned. "You're giving Timmy my Christmas dinner!"

I felt the Iceman's frozen fingers clawing my arm. Another awful chill made me shiver.

"Look," he said, pointing at the Christmas tree.

Mom pulled a big box from under the tree. "Merry Christmas!" she said, handing the present to Timmy. "From the whole Frobisher family."

Timmy read the little card underneath the red bow. "But it says, 'For Kenny.'"

Smiling, Mom ripped the tag off the box and tossed it into the fire. "Oh, that's nothing," she exclaimed. "Kenny never likes anything we give him. He always complains about our presents."

"But that's not true!" I cried.

I felt my heart sink.

It *was* true.

"Come, Kenny," the Iceman ordered. "We must go."

"But how can they do this? We're supposed to have Christmas together! It's not the same without me."

"You are right." His icy blue lips smiled cruelly. "It is *better* without you, Kenny. Much better."

I guess that was true too.

As I looked back, my family opened the rest of their presents. I'd never seen them so happy.

The Iceman grasped my wrist.

I didn't try to pull away. I knew it was hopeless— my family didn't miss me. They didn't even like me!

The Iceman tugged me through the front door again. Outside, a heavy snow began to fall. A blast of icy wind sliced right through me, and I shivered.

The Iceman glided ahead of me.

"I have to talk to you!" I shouted.

But he didn't stop. He floated farther ahead. I walked faster. I had to catch up to him!

The snowflakes whirled around me, stinging my face and my hands. The snow fell thick and fast. I could barely see more than a few feet ahead now.

I'd lost sight of the Iceman completely.

I didn't know which way to go.

I was totally blinded by the whirling, swirling snow.

The wind whipped at my head, my chest, my legs. It blew me back . . . sideways . . . in a circle.

I struggled to walk.

Was I moving forward? I couldn't tell!

I'm lost!

My heartbeat quickened.

I'm frozen and lost.

The Iceman said I would end up like him. A frozen ghost.

Was that what was happening to me?

I spun around, searching frantically for the Iceman.

The winds howled around me. I stumbled in the snow. Fell to the icy ground.

I forced myself to get up. To keep going.

"Iceman! Where are you?" I screamed. "Don't leave me out here alone!"

15

I staggered forward in the icy blizzard.

My feet felt frozen—like two blocks of ice. My hands tingled. I had no feeling in my fingers—none at all.

"Iceman!" I cried. "Iceman! Where are you?"

A strong gust of wind knocked me down. I fell headfirst into a snowbank.

I had to find the Iceman!

I wiped the snow from my face and stared into the storm. Then, on my hands and knees, I crawled through the blizzard.

I crawled and crawled—until I spotted a clearing ahead. A patch where it didn't seem to be snowing!

With my head down, I crawled some more, pushing against the wind.

I crawled until I felt something soft under my hands. Something warm and dry!

I wiped the snow from my cheeks, from my eyelashes. Only it wasn't snow. It was—feathers!

I gazed up.

I was back in Dalby's!

Back in the bedding department—crouched on my hands and knees in the bed!

What is going on?

The bedding department looked as if it had been struck by a blizzard. The curtains, towels, quilts, and bath mats were scattered everywhere—all coated with a white blanket of feathers and foam.

Everything—buried under what looked like a heavy snowfall.

I shuddered.

I knew now that I definitely wasn't dreaming.

Everything that happened was real. Even the ghosts—both of them—were *real ghosts.*

I have to get out of here, fast. Before the third ghost comes.

I swung my feet to the floor—and I started to yawn.

My eyelids drooped.

"No!" I cried. "Not now! Not again!"

I slapped my face. *"Wake up!"* I yelled.

It wasn't working.

I yawned again—and curled up on the bed.

My cheek touched the cool, smooth pillow. "I can't let myself—" I mumbled as my eyes closed.

Then I drifted off to sleep.

WHAM!

I woke with a start and jerked up in the bed.

Bright lights flashed before my eyes!

Red! Yellow! Green!

On and off! On and off!

Crazy music blared.

"Deck your grave with boughs of hemlock!" a high voice shrieked. "Fa-la-la-la-la!"

I checked my wristwatch.

Twelve—midnight!

My heart hammered in my chest.

The third ghost had arrived!

16

I leaped off the bed.

Run! Run for your life!

I tore down the aisle.

I charged through the store. I ran through a department I hadn't been in before. I passed dummies wearing tennis outfits, ski parkas, and bathing suits. The sportswear department.

I skidded to a stop. Could I hide here?

"Stay, Kenny!" someone whispered.

I spun around. "Who—who's there?"

"Don't be a jerk!" A different voice this time. "Get out of here! Now!"

"Who is that? Where are you?"

I broke out into a sweat.

"Why don't you answer me!" I demanded.

I squinted in the darkness. The dim red light of the exit signs cast their eerie glow on everything— the clothes, the counters, the dummies.

The dummies.

I stared hard at the dummies.

They seemed to stare back at me, with dull eyes and blank faces.

I stared at them harder.

I stared at the dummy right next to me—dressed in a golf outfit, holding a golf club.

Then I saw it.

I saw one of its arms begin to move.

I glanced up at its face. A slow smile spread across its lips. Then its club whipped out at me.

I ducked.

The club whizzed by my head. Struck a counter and shattered the glass.

THWAAAK!

It came at me again.

"It's hopeless, Kenny," a dummy behind me whispered. "You're doomed, no matter which way you go!"

I gazed at the dummies in horror.

They stirred and wriggled. They moaned and blinked their eyes.

They were all coming to life!

I staggered backward. "Are you doing this, Iceman? Night Watchman, is it you?"

Or was it the ghost I hadn't met yet? The third ghost.

The dummy in the ski parka stretched out its arms. It moved one stiff leg. Then the other. With rigid, jerky steps, it staggered off the platform.

It headed straight for me. Its glassy eyes stared into my eyes.

Then, in one swift movement, it lifted its ski pole and hurled it at me like a javelin.

I dodged it just in time. The pole grazed my head and slammed into the wall behind me. Stuck there, harpoonlike.

I ran down the aisle—and skidded to a sudden stop.

A group of dummies stood waiting for me. Blocking my path.

"I—I'm not afraid of you," I stammered. "You're just a bunch of dummies."

"I don't think so, Kenny," one of the mannequins chuckled. "We're not dummies—you are the dummy!"

All the dummies broke out into a horrible laugh. Shrieking and laughing—and chanting, "Kenny is a dummy. Kenny is a dummy."

I turned and dashed the other way. I ducked around a corner. All clear. I made a run for it.

"Not so fast, Kenny!" A dummy popped out from behind a counter. He stuck out his stiff, hard leg and tripped me.

"Get away from me!" I shouted as I struggled to my feet.

"Need a hand, Kenny?" the dummy screeched. He unscrewed one of his hands and flung it at me.

I ran and ran.

"You can't leave us, Kenny," a dummy in a bathing suit warned. "We're just starting to have some fun!"

"Kenny is a dummy. Kenny is a dummy." Their hideous, chilling cries echoed through the empty store.

I covered my ears and ran back down the aisle.

Out of the corner of my eye, I saw more of them chasing me. An army of them—marching out of the men's clothing department!

"Kenny is a dummy. Kenny is a dummy," they all chanted.

I ran faster!

Straight toward the toy department—and stopped.

In the dim light, two giant wooden soldiers

twisted their stiff heads. Stretched out their stiff arms. Then stepped forward awkwardly.

They slid their long, golden sabers out of their belts.

They gazed straight at me—and began to march.

Their long, sharp blades whistled as the soldiers sliced the air with them.

"Give up, Kenny!" they screamed. "We know what to do with a monster like you."

Fighting my panic, I turned and ran.

The wooden soldiers chased after me.

"We're going to get you, Kenny!" they shouted. "You don't have a chance!"

I ran faster and faster.

My lungs burned and my legs ached. But I couldn't stop.

I had to get away!

PING!

The sound came from directly in front of me.

The sound of an elevator!

Why hadn't I seen it before?

No time to figure it out.

I ran straight to it. The doors flew open. I jumped in.

The soldiers approached. Only a few feet away now.

I jumped into the elevator. I frantically banged the buttons.

Nothing! The doors wouldn't close.

The soldiers moved in closer.

I hit the buttons again and again.

"Here we come, Kenny!" The soldiers waved their sabers over their heads.

One reached into the elevator and pinned me against the wall.

I pushed and kicked it. I tried to shove it off. It wouldn't let go.

"Hold him!" the other soldier ordered. "Don't let him escape!"

The soldier in the elevator grabbed my arm and yanked it hard, dragging me out.

"No!" I shouted. "Let go! Let go!"

One foot in the elevator, one foot out—I slammed my hand against the buttons.

The elevator doors began to close.

With one mighty yank, I wrenched free of the soldier—just as the doors slammed shut.

I felt the elevator jerk under my feet. I could feel it begin to move. Going down.

Going down.

I stared up at the floor numbers.

The number three lit up.

Would the soldiers take the escalator down?

Would they be there on the first floor? Waiting for me. Ready to attack.

Hurry! Hurry!

I wiped my sweaty palms on my pants.

I hit the button for one again and again.

The light at three went dark.

Two lit up next.

Then one.

I faced the doors—ready to jump out and run.

But the elevator didn't stop. It kept moving. Down. Down. Down.

I pounded on the emergency stop button, but the elevator kept falling.

I swallowed hard.

I felt the elevator picking up speed. Dropping faster and faster.

This can't be! No building in Shadyside had a basement so far down!

The elevator continued to drop—zooming down now.

I crouched down and got ready to crash. I covered my eyes with my hands.

And suddenly it started to slow.

Then it stopped—and the doors swished open.

I stepped out into a narrow room.

In the dim light, I could barely see the brown walls. I felt a damp chill. I choked on a musty smell.

Ping!

I spun around. The elevator was gone! Vanished!

I let out a low groan.

Now what?

I touched a wall. The surface crumbled beneath my fingertips.

Dirt! The wall was made of dirt!

I groped the other three walls. Dirt—all dirt.

I gazed up at the ceiling—but there wasn't one!

The bare branches of a tree swayed overhead. Through the branches, I glimpsed stars and a crescent moon in the night sky.

I turned around slowly, gazing at each dark dirt wall.

Where am I?

Suddenly I knew.

I stood in an open grave.

17

Oh, noooo! *What am I doing in a grave?*

Don't panic, I ordered myself.

Think.

The Fear Street Cemetery is only three blocks from home. That's where I am.

I gazed at the grave walls. If I can climb out of here, I can run home! I can be back in my own house, in my own bed, in minutes.

I dug my fingers into the dirt walls and started climbing. The grave was deep, with really steep walls.

I raised a foot and shoved into a wall. I plunged my fingers into the dirt. Then I heaved myself up.

I planted my other foot in the wall and climbed some more.

I slowly made my way up.

The soil crumpled under my fingertips and fell on my face. Into my eyes. On my lips. I could even taste it on my tongue.

I climbed and climbed.

I was halfway there.

But I had to stop. Something cold, something slimy, wriggled across my hand.

I released my grip and shook my fingers.

Yuck.

A fat, bloated worm flew off.

I began to raise myself up again—but . . .

I felt something slither under my jacket sleeve. Under both sleeves. Down my shirt.

I lost my hold—and plunged to the bottom of the grave.

I tore off my jacket—and screamed.

Worms!

Hundreds of worms slithered around my arms. Slid down my chest. Crept up my legs.

"Get off! Get off me!" I shrieked, shaking my whole body.

The worms crawled up my neck. Up my cheeks. Into my hair.

I shook my head wildly. I jumped up and down. A

clump of worms fell off—but more seemed to take their place.

I clawed at my arms and chest. I brushed the worms frantically from my neck and face.

I heard a sickening plop as their juicy purple bodies fell to the ground.

I grabbed at the dirt, searching for a tree root to hoist myself out.

I found one.

I grabbed on to it and scaled the grave walls. Climbing up, up.

I was almost out.

I peered over the top of the grave.

The moonlight cast a warm, spooky glow over the tombstones. Over the trees. Shadows shifted over the graves. A heavy mist hung in the air.

The cemetery was quiet. Totally silent.

I reached over the top of the grave with both hands.

With all my strength, I began to pull myself out.

But something was wrong.

My leg seemed to be caught.

I gazed down—and gasped.

Stretching up through the dirt, I saw—a hand. A hand gripping my ankle. A bony, skeleton hand!

Its fingers gripped my ankle tighter and tighter. "Noooo!" I screamed.

I kicked and kicked.

The bony fingers dug deeper into my flesh.

"Let me goooo!" I shrieked. I tried to pull myself out—over the edge of the grave.

But the hand pulled me down.

Down.

Down to the bottom of the grave.

18

"Let me goooo!" I screamed again and again.

I clawed at the dirt. Found the tree root.

With all my strength, I dragged myself up. Kicking, kicking, trying to kick free of the skeleton's deadly grip.

I reached the grave opening. Peered over the edge. Started to lift myself out.

My hands began to slip.

I thought I saw something move in the shadows. Was someone out there?

"Help me!" I screamed. "Somebody, help me!"

The bony fingers tugged at my leg. Pulling me harder. Pulling me down.

Something moved out in the cemetery!

This time I was certain.

A figure moved through the mist. I saw it— moving toward me.

"Help me!" I gasped. "Help . . ."

The figure stopped.

"This way!" I screamed. "Help me! You've got to help me!"

The shadowy form moved forward. It heard me! It was coming to save me!

"Hurry!" I cried. "Before it's too late!"

It moved nearer and nearer. It was a man carrying something. A long pole.

The cemetery caretaker—that's who it must be!

Then I saw the long black robe. And the peaked hood almost completely covering his head.

Who was this man?

He approached the edge of the grave—and I screamed.

Five long, bony fingers grasped the pole. The hand of a skeleton. Under the hood, no face. Just a skull with red, glowing eyes!

"The third ghost!" I stammered. "The Ghost of Christmas Future."

The ghost of *my* future.

19

The ghost slowly nodded its head.

Silently, he drew a bony hand from under his robe and raised it in the air. The index finger glowed yellow in the mist.

With his glowing finger, he pointed to the other side of the cemetery.

To three figures coming through the mist. Coming my way.

As they neared, I could see they were kids. About my height. About my age. A boy with curly blond hair. Another boy with short dark hair. A girl with long blond hair.

These kids would help me!

"Over here!" I shouted. "Help! I can't hold on much longer!"

The kids came closer. Slowly.

"Hurry!" I yelled.

They didn't speak.

They didn't quicken their pace.

What's wrong with them? Why aren't they running over here? Why don't they say something?

They came closer.

Something about the way they walked looked strange. So stiff.

Something about their faces looked strange too. Dull and vacant.

"Are you okay?" I shouted up to them. "Are you guys in trouble too?"

The kids stopped at the edge of the grave.

I peered up into their faces—and they began to hum.

Softly at first.

Then louder. More like moaning now.

The boy with the blond hair stood closest to me. "Help me! Give me your hand!" I called out to him.

He didn't answer.

Their moaning grew louder.

Then, suddenly, it stopped—and the kids began to laugh. And as they did, their faces began to change.

Their eyes bulged out.

Their lips turned black and scaly.

Their skin began to rot away.

I stared in horror as slimy mucus oozed from their pores.

A foul stench drifted down toward me. The stench of their decaying flesh.

Monsters!

They were monsters!

Hideous monsters!

20

"**M**onsters!" I cried, glancing away from their terrifying faces.

"Look, Kenny!" they shrieked in unison. "Look at us!"

"I—I can't," I stammered.

The monsters shrieked with laughter. The girl monster pushed her hideous face close to mine. "Aren't I beautiful?" she grinned, revealing a row of black, rotted teeth.

"Answer her!" the blond-haired boy ordered.

"You're—you're the most disgusting thing I've ever seen!" I choked out.

"You'll change your mind soon," the brown-haired monster hooted. "When you look just like us!"

His eyeballs rolled back in his bulging eye sockets and disappeared totally.

"Never!" I shrieked. "I'll never look like you!"

"Live a monster. Die a monster. Live a monster. Die a monster," the three hideous creatures began to chant.

They lowered themselves to the edge of the grave. Their stench filled my nostrils. I started to gag.

"Go away!" I shouted. "Leave me alone!"

"Thought you wanted our help," the brown-haired boy chuckled.

"Help me. Somebody helllp meeee," the girl mimicked me. "Hur-rry!"

The monsters burst out laughing.

I glanced at the ghost. He held up his glowing finger and the laughter abruptly stopped.

"We used to be just like you!" one of the monsters said. "We loved being mean."

"Just like you. Just like you," the three monsters chanted.

The three monsters giggled.

"You are our past," the girl rasped. "But we are your future!"

"Oh, noooo!" I moaned.

Now I understood.

That woman in Dalby's called me a monster.
And the wooden soldiers did too.
Live a monster. Die a monster.
Now I definitely understood.
I stared up at the third ghost.
He pointed his glowing finger at me.
He was going to turn me into a monster—for real.
The ghost brushed his finger across my cheek.
"Noooo!" I begged. "Don't!
"Please, please! Give me a second chance! I'll do anything! Anything! I'll change. I'll be . . . good!"

21

"**P**lease!" I screamed. "Please! Please!"

"Calm down, son!" A light flashed on above me. "Believe me. There's nothing to get upset about!"

Someone grabbed my arm. I opened my eyes. It was a security guard. A Dalby's security guard.

"The door jams now and then," the guard explained as he led me out of the closet.

A crowd of shoppers gathered around us. I could see Santa's Village just ahead.

"It took us a while to realize you were in there," the guard continued as he patted me on the shoulder. "With all the noise out here, it was hard to hear you yelling!"

I glanced back over my shoulder at the computer control room. The guard reached back and closed the door.

I checked my wristwatch: 7:50.

I checked the date window: 12-24.

"Is it still Christmas Eve?" I asked—just to make sure.

"Of course it's Christmas Eve," he replied with a puzzled look. "But the store closes in ten minutes. If we hadn't found you now, you might have been here right through Christmas Day!"

I glanced down Santa Street.

I saw Santa give the last kid in line a candy cane.

The kid beamed a smile from ear to ear!

I saw all the cheerful little elves gather around the Christmas tree to sing one last Christmas carol.

I'd never seen anything so wonderful in my whole life.

"Your mom and sister thought you'd left without them," the guard went on. "So they went home. You'd better hurry back, before they start to worry about you!"

"Right, I'd better hurry!" I agreed.

I checked my watch again: 7:55.

Only five minutes till the store closed.

Was it enough time?

I raced over to the doll display.

I had to find that cute little ballerina doll! Kristi never did finish telling Santa about it. And it was my fault. If I didn't give it to her, who would?

I spotted the doll at the bottom of a pile of dolls. I snapped it up and ran over to a salesclerk.

"How much is this doll?" I asked.

"Oh, that one is ten dollars," the lady said pleasantly. "Isn't she beautiful?"

I let out a sigh.

I reached into my pocket—even though I knew I had only a five-dollar bill.

"Do you have a smaller doll? One that costs five dollars?" I asked the clerk as I unfolded the bill.

I glanced down—and gasped with surprise.

In my hand I held a ten-dollar bill!

"Here you are!" I exclaimed, handing her the money. "I can buy this doll after all. Merry Christmas!"

"Merry Christmas to you too." The woman smiled. She dropped the doll in a bag and carefully reached over the counter to give it to me.

I raced through the store.

"Merry Christmas!" I shouted, and waved as I glided down the escalator. "Merry Christmas, everybody!"

"It's Kenny Frobisher," I heard a woman exclaim.

"No, it can't be," another woman said. "Kenny Frobisher never said anything nice to anyone."

"But it *is* me," I shouted. "And a happy new year too!" I exclaimed as I dashed out the store.

22

I ran all the way home, hugging the shopping bag that held Kristi's gift.

As I dashed down Fear Street, I saw the Christmas wreaths on all our neighbors' doors. Through their windows, I could see their Christmas trees all lit up. They looked so beautiful!

But the most beautiful tree stood in the big front window at 27 Fear Street. My house.

I knocked hard on the front door. Mom flung it open.

"Kenny!" she exclaimed. "There you are!" Her face lit up with a huge smile. "I was so worried about you, honey!"

"Merry Christmas, Mom!" I greeted her. I jumped inside and ran into the living room.

The Christmas tree, the roaring fire in the fireplace, the Christmas music—it was all perfect. Just the way Christmas Eve is supposed to be.

Dad sat in front of the tree. There was an old book on his lap. Mom sat down next to Kristi in front of the fireplace.

On the coffee table sat a tray with mugs of steaming hot chocolate and a plate of homemade cookies.

"Sorry, Kenny," Dad said softly. "We were reading *A Christmas Carol.* I know how you hate it."

"Not anymore, Dad," I said, shaking my head. I grabbed a mug of hot chocolate and flopped down on the couch. "I love it! It's one of my favorite stories now!"

Laughing, Dad shook his head. "Since when, Kenny?" he asked. "How did that happen?"

I took a sip from my mug and snuggled into the couch pillows. "It's a long story, Dad," I replied.

And a scary one.

One I'll never forget.

The next morning I jumped out of bed and snapped open the window shade.

Wow!

A ton of snow had fallen on Shadyside overnight. It sparkled and glistened in the bright morning sun. Fear Street looked like a Christmas card.

"Kenny, are you awake yet?" Mom called. She poked her head in the doorway. "Is Rags with you? I can't find him."

"Rags? Here, boy!" I called.

I searched my room. I checked under the bed, then inside the closet. No sign of him in any of his usual hiding places.

"He's not here, Mom."

"I guess we'll just have to keep looking," Mom sighed. "Kristi is so upset. If we don't find him soon, it will ruin her whole Christmas."

"He came back last time, didn't he?"

"Last time?" Mom asked. She frowned at me. "We've never lost Rags before."

I watched Mom close the door and remembered everything all in a rush.

The Night Watchman.

The Iceman.

The ghost in the Fear Street Cemetery.

The three gruesome monsters . . .

I shuddered.

I gazed around my room. At my bed, my posters,

103

my electric guitar—just to remind myself that it had all been a dream! A nightmare. The worst I'd ever had!

I pulled on a sweatshirt and jeans. Then I dashed downstairs. In the kitchen I found Kristi kneeling beside Rags's little bed.

"He'll come back," I promised her.

She peered up at me and I saw the tears in her eyes. "What if he never comes back?" she whispered. "What if he's lost? What if a car . . ."

"Don't worry, Kristi." I patted her on the shoulder. "He's okay. He'll be home any minute."

Would Rags come home? I didn't know. But I had to say something, didn't I?

The doorbell rang.

"I'll answer it," I called out.

I pulled open the door and found Timmy Smathers standing on our porch.

He was holding a leash.

Just like in my dream!

"Look who I found!" Timmy exclaimed. He stepped aside and Rags dashed by him, into our living room.

"Rags!" Kristi squealed.

"Woof! Woof!" Rags barked as he leaped into Kristi's arms.

"I found him behind our house," Timmy explained. "I brought him right over."

"Gee, thanks, Timmy. You're really a nice guy. I guess I never told you that before."

Timmy looked at me uncertainly. Not that I blamed him. I felt my cheeks turn red with embarrassment.

"Is this some kind of trick?" he asked suspiciously. "You're not hiding a water gun behind your back, are you?"

"It's not a trick, Timmy," I replied. "From now on, things are going to be different," I promised. "I'm not going to play any mean tricks on you, or anyone else—ever again."

"You're not?" Timmy asked, shocked. "What happened to you?"

"You could say I had a bad dream," I said. "And finally I woke up!"

I saw Kristi poking around the presents under the Christmas tree. I remembered that I hadn't wrapped up her doll yet.

"Hey, Timmy. Come in the kitchen a second," I whispered. "I have to wrap something."

"Sure," he answered. Timmy followed me to the pantry, where I had hidden Kristi's doll. I started to wrap it.

"Kristi is going to be so happy when she sees this!" I said, winding a piece of shiny red ribbon around the box.

"Gee, Kenny." Timmy sighed as he watched me. "I guess that dream really did change you." He placed his finger on the ribbon so I could tie a bow.

"Thanks," I replied as I fumbled with ribbon ends.

I glanced down at the box as I started to make a knot—and gulped.

Timmy's finger.

As bony as a skeleton finger.

I finished the bow quickly.

I glanced up just as Timmy placed his finger thoughtfully to his chin.

My jaw dropped in horror.

Timmy's finger glowed!

I stared into his eyes. They glowed too. An eerie red.

Timmy grinned. He pulled up the big peaked hood of his black parka. In the shadow of his hood, his face looked ghastly pale. His cheeks turned to sunken purple hollows.

"Y-you!" I stammered. "You're the third ghost. It wasn't a dream! I—I don't believe it!"

"Why not, Kenny?" he replied in a ghostly voice. "You live on Fear Street. What did you expect?"

Timmy pulled open the kitchen door and strolled out.

He glanced over his shoulder and waved his bony hand.

"Merry Christmas to all," he cried out with a deep, ghoulish laugh. "And to all a good fright!"

Are you ready for another walk
down Fear Street?
Turn the page for a terrifying
sneak preview.

DON'T EVER GET SICK
AT GRANNY'S

Coming mid-December 1996.

"AH-CHOO!"

I sneezed so hard my body slammed into the back of the chair. Granny Marsha took a step toward me.

"Sneezes are a warning," Granny said. "Of *bad* things to come."

"I'm okay! Really!" I cried, struggling to my feet. "I have allergies! I'm allergic to your cats."

Granny Marsha squinted those cold gray eyes at me again. "I don't have a cat. You know that."

"Of course," I bluffed. "Then it must be the dust."

"There's no dust in Granny's house," she countered. She raised her hand. Slowly. Very slowly. "Dust wouldn't be good for Granny's patients."

Patients! What patients?

Granny moved closer and closer. Her hand went higher and higher. My eyes grew wide with fright. Suddenly her hand came speeding toward my head. She was going to hit me!

No! I flung my arms up, shielding my face from the blow.

"Corey! You act like I'm going to strike you," Granny scolded. "Would Granny do a thing like that?" She shook her head. "I just want to feel your forehead."

"Oh. Right." I chuckled nervously and lowered my hands. "Go ahead. But I'm totally fine."

She pressed her hand against my forehead. "I don't know—you seem a little warm." She made little clucking noises. "*Too* warm, if you ask me."

I jerked backward. "I'm fine. I'm terrific. I'm just overheated from riding in that hot car. You know," I explained, "the air-conditioning broke down."

Granny folded her arms across her chest. "Just to be safe, I'll keep my eye on you for the rest of the day."

She wasn't kidding.

I spent the afternoon watching videos, and Granny Marsha spent the afternoon watching me. She never left her chair once.

Every time I'd turn to take a sip of my drink, or grab a handful of popcorn, there she was. Staring at me.

"Are you sick yet?" she'd ask with a hopeful smile. It was like she *wanted* me to be sick. She was really giving me the creeps.

Pretty soon I didn't even have to turn around to know she was looking at me. I could feel her eyes drilling holes in the back of my neck.

To make matters worse, that tickling feeling I had in my nose had moved to my throat. And my eyes were getting watery and itchy.

I stared at the TV, but I couldn't really concentrate. Dad's warning kept ringing in my ears.

"Don't ever get sick at Granny's," he told me. Why not? What did he mean?

I'm *not* sick, I told myself. I'm nervous. Granny is making me a nervous wreck.

I sneaked a look at her out of the corner of my eye. She sat hunched over with her chin stuck out, staring at me. A vulture. That's what she looks like, I thought. One of those cartoon vultures.

"Don't you have stuff you need to do?" I asked.

"It can wait," she replied, narrowing her eyelids

to little squinty slits in her face. "*I* can wait. Granny's good at waiting."

I shuddered.

Two hours later Granny called into the living room. "Dinner! It's time to feed that cold," she said, leading me into the kitchen.

"But I don't have a cold," I protested, sitting down at the kitchen table.

"We'll see about that," Granny gushed.

We ate roast chicken and dumplings. Or I did. She barely touched her food, she was so busy watching me.

"I think this is the best chicken I've ever eaten," I said heartily. I wanted to sound really healthy. "I could probably eat a whole chicken by myself."

Granny didn't seem to go for it. She pursed her lips. "Hmmmm," was all she said.

Hmmmm. What did that mean?

Granny continued to stare.

She made me so nervous my hands started to shake. I could barely raise my fork to my mouth.

"You know, you look very pale." Granny leaned across the table with her hand stretched toward my forehead. "*Too* pale."

"I'm always pale," I fibbed, leaning out of her reach. "I'm a very pale person."

Granny Marsha raised an eyebrow.

"I was voted most pale in my class." I held up one hand. "Honest."

She reached out to feel my forehead again, but I thrust my plate into her hands. "Chicken! Chicken makes me pale. And boy, was that good chicken! I bet I ate three helpings at least."

Granny carried our plates to the sink. While she loaded them in the dishwasher, I bolted for the bathroom.

"Can't look pale," I muttered, closing the bathroom door. I hurried to the mirror. "Pale means sick and I don't know why, but I *can't* get sick at Granny's."

I slapped my cheeks and pinched them to give them color. Then I peered at my reflection in the mirror above the sink.

"Oh, great." I wasn't pale anymore. Now my face was red and blotchy. I didn't look healthier. I looked like I had a rash!

I tried splashing water on my face, but it didn't seem to help, either.

"Are you all right in there?" Granny's voice called from outside the bathroom door.

"Uh, yes, Granny," I replied. I put a big healthy smile on my face and opened the door.

"I'd better show you to your room," Granny said. "We'll need plenty of sleep, if we're going to fight that cold."

"Sleep. That's what I need." I bobbed my head in agreement. "I've been up since five. I'm beat."

Granny led me up the stairs to the second floor.

Show me my room and then leave me alone, I thought. I followed Granny into a small room under one of the eaves of the house. It was like a pirate's hideout. The headboard of the bed was painted with sailing ships. The dresser looked like a sea captain's trunk. And the wall was hung with fishing nets and a giant stuffed marlin.

"Cool room." I nodded my approval.

"I'm sure you'll be very happy here," Granny said, turning down the bedcover. "Just remember, if you do get sick"—she slowly turned her head to look at me—*"I know how to take care of you."*

Her lips curled into that wacko smile again.

Why did she keep saying that? How would she take care of me? I shuddered. She was really giving me the creeps.

Finally Granny left the room. I put on my pajamas and collapsed on my bed. All those hours with that weirdo watching me had stressed me out.

I want to sleep for the whole weekend, I thought. Until Mom and Dad get back.

But I couldn't sleep. Dad's warning kept running through my head. *"Don't get sick at Granny's. Whatever you do—DON'T GET SICK."*

"I won't get sick," I mumbled to myself. I pulled the covers up under my chin and stared at the peeling plaster on the ceiling. "I won't get sick."

I repeated those words over and over. Finally I drifted off into a restless sleep.

A beam of sunlight hit me in the face, and I shot up from the bed. "Morning already?" I exclaimed. "It can't be."

I tried to swallow. My throat was sore. I sniffed. My nose was running. I had chills.

"Oh, no!" I groaned. "I'm sick!"

Something moved in the corner of my room.

I froze.

About R. L. Stine

R. L. Stine, the creator of *Ghosts of Fear Street*, has written almost 100 scary novels for kids. The *Ghosts of Fear Street* series, like the *Fear Street* series, takes place in Shadyside and centers on the scary events that happen to people on Fear Street.

When he isn't writing, R. L. Stine likes to play pinball on his very own pinball machine, and explore New York City with his wife, Jane, and fifteen-year-old son, Matt.

R·L·STINE

Is The Roller Coaster Really Haunted?

THE BEAST

❑ 88055-1/$3.99

It Was An Awsome Ride—Through Time!

THE BEAST 2

❑ 52951-X/$3.99

A MINSTREL® BOOK
Published by Pocket Books